IT'S KWANZAA TIME!

IT'S KWANZAA TIME!

LINDA AND CLAY GOSS

with illustrations by

Ashley Bryan ▲ Carole Byard

Floyd Cooper ▲ Leo and Diane Dillon ▲ Jan Spivey Gilchrist

Jonathan Green ▲ Jerry Pinkney

G. P. PUTNAM'S SONS
New York

To our children: Aisha, Uhuru, and Jamaal
To the Educators to Africa, of Philadelphia, PA,
and to the National Association of Black Storytellers

We thank the following people for their support, advice, understanding, patience, assistance,
encouragement, and kindness: Pat Gauch, Shelly Cameron, Carla Glasser, Laura Walsh,
Carole Weathers, Rafael Ramos, and Momma.
Asante sana—a special thank you to Maulana Karenga for establishing Kwanzaa.

Text copyright © 1994, 1995 by Linda and Clay Goss
Illustration page 11 copyright © 1995 by Ashley Bryan
Illustration page 18 copyright © 1995 by Carole Byard
Illustration page 23 copyright © 1995 by Leo and Diane Dillon
Illustration page 35 copyright © 1995 by Jerry Pinkney
Illustration page 43 copyright © 1994, 1995 by Jonathan Green
Illustration page 51 copyright © 1995 by Floyd Cooper
Illustration page 55 copyright © 1995 by Jan Spivey Gilchrist
G. P. Putnam's Sons, a division of Penguin Putnam Books for Young Readers,
345 Hudson Street, New York, NY 10014.
First paperback edition, 2002.
G. P. Putnam's Sons, Reg. U. S. Pat. & Tm. Off. Published simultaneously in Canada.
Manufactured in China by South China Printing Co. Ltd. The text is set in Souvenir Light.

Library of Congress Cataloging-in-Publication Data
Goss, Linda. It's Kwanzaa time! / by Linda and Clay Goss. p. cm. Includes bibliographical references.
Summary: Stories, recipes, and activities introduce the holiday of Kwanzaa and the ways in which it is
celebrated. 1. Kwanzaa—Juvenile literature. [1. Kwanzaa. 2. Afro-Americans—Social life and customs.]
1. Goss, Clay. II. Title. GT4403.G67 1995 92-30380 394.2'68—dc20 CIP AC

"Rosa Parks, a Woman of Courage" first appeared in *Rosa Parks* © 1973 by Eloise Greenfield,
published by HarperCollins Publishers
"The Nguzo Saba" appears in *Kwanzaa: A Celebration of Family, Community and Culture* © 1998 by Maulana Karenga
published by University of Sankore Press.
ISBN 0-399-23956-1
3 5 7 9 10 8 6 4 2

CONTENTS

THE NGUZO SABA
(The Seven Principles)

1. *Umoja* (Unity) To strive for and maintain unity in the family, community, nation, and race

2. *Kujichagulia* (Self-determination) To define ourselves, name ourselves, create for ourselves, and speak for ourselves instead of being defined, named, created for, and spoken for by others

3. *Ujima* (Collective Work and Responsibility) To build and maintain our community together and make our sisters' and brothers' problems our problems and to solve them together

4. *Ujamaa* (Cooperative Economics) To build and maintain our own stores, shops, and other businesses and to profit from them together

5. *Nia* (Purpose) To make our collective vocation the building and developing of our community in order to restore our people to their traditional greatness

6. *Kuumba* (Creativity) To do always as much as we can, in the way we can, in order to leave our community more beautiful and beneficial than we inherited it

7. *Imani* (Faith) To believe with all our heart in our people, our parents, our teachers, our leaders, and the righteousness and victory of our struggle

Maulana Karenga

INTRODUCTION

Jambo watoto. Hello children, and friends, too:

Habari Gani? What's the news? It's Kwanzaa time! You and your family are cordially invited to join us in a celebration of Kwanzaa, an African-American holiday.

Please bring your imagination and your curiosity with you. We hope our book, *It's Kwanzaa Time!* will provide the other things you need to enjoy this exciting holiday.

As you turn the pages of this book, please feel free to sing, dance, laugh, and jump for joy.

Kwanzaa is a relatively new African-American celebration, yet it is based on ancient African festivals and customs. To celebrate Kwanzaa is to create a warm cultural stew, mixing and blending African traditions with African-American customs, Afro-Caribbean customs, and Afro-Latin customs.

Maulana Karenga conceived and developed the idea for Kwanzaa in 1966. He established seven important principles called the *Nguzo Saba* and seven main symbols. He wanted to enrich cultural harmony and pride. The principles and symbols come from the Kiswahili language. The word Kwanzaa comes from the phrase "Matunda Ya Kwanza," which means "first fruits." Maulana Karenga added the extra "a" at the end of *Kwanzaa* so the word would have seven letters to go with the seven principles and symbols. Kiswahili, commonly called Swahili, is spoken by over 50 million people in East Africa. African languages such as Yoruba, which is spoken in Nigeria, and Twi, which is spoken in Ghana, are also used during Kwanzaa time.

The seven days of Kwanzaa are celebrated from December 26 through January 1. Each day a candle representing a symbol is lit, and one of the seven principles is discussed. Many community groups, however, celebrate the holiday in a large gathering usually held in a home, church, or school. During this ceremony all the candles are lit and all of the seven principles are discussed. This book is based on one of those community gatherings. Since 1976, Linda, one of the authors, has conducted a Kwanzaa program hosted by the Educators to Africa, of Philadelphia, Pennsylvania. It is one of the largest gatherings in the city. Hundreds and hundreds of people of all ages wearing African garb come together to give thanks, share memories, and celebrate their African heritage.

It's Kwanzaa Time! is designed to put sparkle in your imaginations and warmth in your hearts.

We encourage you to explore the different ways in which you can make Kwanzaa special in your life. Rejoice!

Baki na heri, Remain in peace,
Linda and Clay Goss

CALL YOUR FATHER!
CALL YOUR MOTHER!
CALL YOUR SISTER!
CALL YOUR BROTHER!
IT'S KWANZAA TIME. FAMILY TIME.
IT'S KWANZAA TIME. FAMILY TIME.

It's December 26, the first day of Kwanzaa. Knock! Knock! Folks are knocking at the door. They are clad in African gowns and dashikis. They are carrying bags of handmade gifts under their arms and holding sweet-smelling covered dishes in their hands. An African-American family is celebrating Kwanzaa tonight. The father and mother of the house open the door and greet the folks in Swahili, *"Habari Gani?"* they say, which means, What is the day? The folks reply, *"Umoja!"* which means Unity, the first day of Kwanzaa. The folks enter and are surrounded by friendly men, women, and children who hug them. Loved ones and honored guests of all ages and shades of brown have gathered in this home tonight. The home is filled with Kwanzaa colors: red, black, and green. A banner saying "Happy Kwanzaa" stretches across the threshold. Ribbons, streamers, and cards hang from the windows. A large poster displaying the *Nguzo Saba*, the seven principles of Kwanzaa, decorates the wall. A red, black, and green flag called the *Bendera Ya Taifa* hangs above the doorway.

DOON, DOON, DOON, DOON, DOON, DA-DOON!

The drums summon the gathering. It is time for the Kwanzaa ceremony to begin. The people join hands and gather around the Kwanzaa symbols, which are placed on a large table draped in strips of kente cloth, a multicolored fabric from Ghana. There is:

- Mazao *(mah-zah-o):* a straw basket of fruits and vegetables that represents our roots and the rewards of our labors.
- Mkeka *(mm-kee-kah):* a place mat, usually made of straw, that symbolizes the foundation of our traditions and history.
- Kinara *(kah-nah-rah):* a wooden candle holder that holds the seven candles and symbolizes our ancestors.
- Muhindi *(moo-heen-dee):* ears of corn that symbolize our children.
- Zawadi *(zah-wah-dee):* gifts that have been made by hand, or a book that represents knowledge.
- Kikombe Cha Umoja *(kee-koom-bay cha OO-mo-jah):* a wooden goblet that symbolizes unity and is used to pour libation.

In the center is:

- Mishumaa Saba *(mee-shoo-mah sah-bah):* the seven candles that will be placed in the Kinara. There is one black candle, three red candles, and three green candles. The Mishumaa Saba symbolizes the Nguzo Saba, the seven principles of Kwanzaa. The candles are lighted, one by one, each night of Kwanzaa so that on the seventh night, all seven candles are lighted.

The mother and father of the house welcome the people and introduce one of the honored guests, a poet who performs the libation. The libation is the pouring of water on the ground; the act symbolizes respect for the ancestors. The poet picks up the Kikombe Cha Umoja, the unity cup, and points it first to the North wind, then to the East wind, the South wind, and the West wind. He speaks in Yoruba, a language spoken by the Yoruba people in Nigeria. He pauses after each phrase and slowly pours the water.

Iba Olodumare.	I respect the Creator.
Iba Orisha.	I respect the deified ancestors.
Iba Baba mi ati iya mi lai lai.	I respect all my grandmothers and grandfathers back to the beginning.

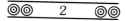

Iba Bab mi ati iya mi.   I respect my mother and my father.

Iba Orimi.   I respect the spirit of God in me.

Iba Ọmọnde.   I respect the children who are coming.

A singer, another honored guest, teaches the children a song about Kwanzaa.

It's Kwanzaa Time

Call your Father!
Call your Mother!
Call your Sister!
Call your Brother!

It's Kwanzaa time. Family time.
It's Kwanzaa time. Family time.

Black people pulling together—Harambee
Trying to make things better—Harambee
Seven days and seven nights
Seven candles we will light
Seven candles we will light.

Green is for the land.
Red is for the blood.
Black is for the people
Whom we love.

It's Kwanzaa time. Family time.
It's Kwanzaa time. Family time.

The first fruits mean Kwanzaa.
We'll say the Nguzo Saba
From Umoja to Imani
Love! Joy! and Harmony!
Love! Joy! and Harmony!

Gather Mkeka!
Gather Kinara!
Gather Kikombe
Gather Mishumaa!

It's Kwanzaa time. Family time.
It's Kwanzaa time. Family time.

Mazao, Muhindi we will take.
Zawadi, the gifts we will make
We'll see you at the Karamu
Habari gani to all of you.
Habari gani to all of you.

It's Kwanzaa time. Family time.
It's Kwanzaa time. Family time.

The drums beat: DA-DOON! DOON! DOON! DA-DOON! DOON! DOON!

The Mishumaa Saba, the seven candles, are lighted. The black candle is lit first, then the red candle glows, then the green candle glows, then another red candle glows, then another green candle glows, then another red candle glows, and another green candle glows. What a beautiful sight! Warm, glowing candlelight! The gathering sings:

This Little Light   *Traditional*

This little light of mine—
    I'm gonna let it shine.
This little light of mine—
    I'm gonna let it shine.
This little light of mine—
    I'm gonna let it shine.
Let it shine. Let it shine. Let it shine.

Everywhere I go—
    I'm gonna let it shine.

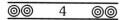

Everywhere I go—
    I'm gonna let it shine.
Everywhere I go—
    I'm gonna let it shine.
Let it shine. Let it shine. Let it shine.

The historian, another honored guest, leads the group in chanting the Nguzo Saba, the seven Kwanzaa principles:

Umoja *(oo-mo-jah)*

Kujichagulia *(koo-gee-chah-goo-lee-ah)*

Ujima *(oo-jee-mah)*

Ujamaa *(oo-jah-mah)*

Nia *(nee-ah)*

Kuumba *(koo-oom-bah)*

Imani *(ee-mah-nee)*

The children listen carefully as the historian explains the meaning of the Nguzo Saba.

Umoja means Unity.

Kujichagulia means Self-determination.

Ujima means Collective Work and Responsibility.

Ujamaa means Cooperative Economics.

Nia means Purpose.

Kuumba means Creativity.

Imani means Faith.

The historian asks, "Who is the founder of Kwanzaa?"

"Maulana Karenga!" the children answer.

Then the Kikombe Cha Umoja, the unity cup, is passed around. Everyone makes a ceremonial gesture of drinking from it. This symbolizes unity and harmony in the group. When the cup has been passed around the circle, everyone shouts:

HARAMBEE! HARAMBEE! HARAMBEE! HARAMBEE! HARAMBEE! HARAMBEE! HARAMBEE!

Harambee *(hah-ram-bay)* means pulling together. They sing:

> We are pulling together.
> We are pulling together.
> We are pulling together.
> Oh yes we are.

The children sit on the floor. The adults form a circle around them. A Zawadi, the Kwanzaa gift, is given to every child. One by one the adults call out the name of a heroine or hero.

Names such as Harriet Tubman, Frederick Douglass, Sojourner Truth, Martin Luther King, Jr., Rosa Parks, Malcolm X, Marian Anderson, and Nelson Mandela echo throughout the room. The children thank the adults for the gifts and their words of wisdom. The grown-ups sit down with the children. The drums play loudly:

DA-DOON DA-DOON DA-DOON DOON DOON DOON

Another honored guest is introduced. She is the storyteller. The storyteller is wearing a pretty, long flowing gown made of African fabric. She is carrying a quilted bag, which she calls her "story bag." In it are bells and story cloths. She reaches into her story bag and pulls out some bells. The storyteller rings the bells, walks around the circle, and greets the family gathering by chanting several times:

STORY! STORYTELLING TIME! STORY! STORYTELLING TIME! STORY! STORYTELLING TIME! STORY! STORYTELLING TIME!

"I have seven stories to tell. There are seven stories for the seven candles of Kwanzaa, and I will tell you one story now."

And so unfolds the first day of Kwanzaa.

SEVEN STORIES FOR KWANZAA

F I R S T   D A Y

Black candle
December 26, first day of Kwanzaa
Principle: Umoja (unity)
Symbol: Mazao (straw basket of fruit)

▼

I am going to tell you a story about a family. The people in this story do not have names. But do not worry about that, because this is an old story based on an Aesop fable. In an Aesop tale we listen to what is going on and what is being said, rather than what names the characters have and where they are. Aesop tells us many things about ourselves, and that is why the fables have been passed down and handed from parents to children and from their children to their children, going from country to country, each telling reflecting the teller's culture. Telling fables in the home brings the family closer together. That is what Umoja, unity, is all about, that is what this Aesop fable is all about, and so I pass it on to you.

THE SEVEN CHILDREN—UMOJA

Illustration by Ashley Bryan

A farmer and his wife had seven children. Now, folks from neighboring farms were always telling them how well-blessed they were to have such fine, healthy children.

But sometimes the farmer and his wife didn't feel quite so lucky because the seven children constantly argued and fought with each other. They yelled and screamed at the top of their voices. They threw stools and bowls across the room. Sounds of screams and things crashing into walls could be heard all day and sometimes even all night. At suppertime, when the family gathered at the table, the seven children made faces at one another and kicked at each other's feet. There was no peace in the farmer's home.

One evening, for supper, the farmer's wife cooked everyone's favorite meal—chicken and dumpling stew. She placed the big pot of stew in the middle of the long table and announced, "It's time to eat."

The farmer and the seven children rushed to the table as they always did, and blessed the food. Slowly, the mother served the farmer his bowl of stew. The farmer served a bowl of stew to his wife. None of the seven children could wait their turn for a bowl of stew. They grabbed the pot, yanked it this way and that, and flung it to the wall. All the delicious-looking chicken and dumplings spilled out onto the floor.

The farmer pounded on the table and shouted, "Enough is enough! Clean up the mess you have made and go to bed." The seven children began to cry and blame one another.

Later that night, the farmer and his wife couldn't sleep. "I'm worried about our children," said the wife.

"They are certainly a wild bunch, but I believe buried in their hearts is kindness," said the farmer.

"You are right, my dear husband, but we need a way to dig up that treasure buried beneath their hearts," said the wife.

Early the next morning, the farmer woke up each of the seven children. "Hurry and do your chores, children, for we are going on a journey through the woods," said the farmer.

The seven children were full of anticipation. They loved walking through the woods. Quickly, they did their chores and ran to the table to eat their morning meal. But, instead of finding seven bowls of hot rice, they saw seven neatly tied bundles lying on the table. "Where is our food?" asked the seven children.

"It's time to go on our journey," said the father. "We will eat fruits and berries along the way."

"Oh, goody," shouted the children.

"And take these bundles with you," said their mother. "Don't open them now, for you will need them later." She gave each of the seven children a bundle and a hug. And so, off they went.

The farmer led his seven children through a part of the forest that was unfamiliar to them. There were no clear-cut walkways. They saw one fruit tree, but it bore very little fruit. They saw only one sweet berry bush, but it was surrounded by a thicket of thorns. Mosquitoes buzzed around their ears. Snakes glided across their path. They walked all day long. When they came to a clearing, the farmer and the seven children stopped to rest. The farmer said to them, "My dear children, I must return home at once. There is something out here your mother and I want all of you to find. When you have it, you will be able to return home."

"But, Father," said one of the seven children, "the sun is going down."

The farmer said no more and walked away.

"What shall we do now?" said one of the seven children.

"I will decide, because I am the oldest," said the oldest child.

"But I am the smartest. I should decide what we should do," said the child next to the oldest one.

"I'm hungry," said the child before the child in the middle.

"I'm thirsty," said the child in the middle.

"I'm scared," said the child after the child in the middle.

"My legs hurt," said the child next to the youngest child.

"I want to go home," said the youngest child, and he cried as loudly as he could.

The seven children began arguing over which direction to take and what should be done next and who should be doing it!

One of the seven children claimed that he knew what their mother and father wanted them to find, but he wasn't going to tell any of them.

Each of the seven children was curious about what was in the others' bundles, but no one wanted to share the contents with anyone else. Finally each of the seven children ran off into the woods in a different direction, hoping to get as far away from the others as possible.

When she was safely away, the oldest child opened up her bundle and found two flint stones. The child next to the oldest child opened up his bundle and found kindling, bits and pieces of dry sticks and twigs. One of the seven children found a net made of tiny strings in his bundle. Another one of the children unfolded a large quilted blanket that was inside her bundle. The middle child discovered a canteen of water in her bundle. The child next to the youngest child had a bundle wrapped within a bundle within a bundle. Inside the last bundle she saw a loaf of banana bread. The youngest child was very confused because he had found a piece of cloth inside his bundle. Something was drawn on the cloth but he could not tell what it was because the woods had become dark and strange animal sounds could be heard. The youngest child screamed out in terror. The other children, fearing that their brother was in danger, ran through the woods to help him. Then he showed them what he had found in his bundle.

"We will need to make a fire with my flint stones so we can see what is on the piece of cloth," said the oldest child.

"I will help you, my sister. I have some kindling," said the child next to the oldest child.

After they had made the fire, they set the net up like a tent so the mosquitoes wouldn't bite them. They passed the canteen around so each of them could drink some water. The child next to the youngest child gave each of her brothers and sisters a piece of banana bread. They looked at the piece of cloth and realized that it was a map showing them how to get back home.

Feeling somewhat better, they lay under the blanket and went to sleep. The next morning, the seven children woke up. They felt strong and happy.

They were glad they had stayed together and were able to make it through the night without harm coming to any of them.

The seven children followed the directions on the map and returned home through the woods safely. The farmer and his wife were pleased to see their children. Holding hands, the family formed a circle and gave thanks to their creator. Then the children told their mother and father how each one of their brothers and sisters had shared what was in the bundles.

"Oh, children, did you find the thing your dear mother and I wanted you to find?"

"Yes, Father," said the oldest of the seven children. "Together we used what we had been given and found our way out of the forest. We found unity."

The youngest of the seven children spoke up. "Yes, but we also found Mother's delicious banana bread!"

The father, mother, and all the children laughed. The father looked around at his family enjoying each other and feeling happy that they were together again. He said, "We are together as a family; this is our strength. Together we have found unity."

Red candle
December 27, second day of Kwanzaa
Principle: Kujichagulia (self-determination)
Symbol: Mkeka (straw mat)

In meeting Rosa Parks, one sees a small, delicate-looking woman who has a soft voice and a beautiful smile. Her gentle presence fills a room with warmth and kindness. Yet Rosa Parks is a woman who was not afraid to speak up. She was determined to fight for her civil rights. She spoke out against the unfair seating on the buses in Montgomery, Alabama, where African-Americans had to sit at the rear of the bus. Many people call Rosa Parks the "mother of the Civil Rights Movement," because her courage and determination led to Congress passing the Civil Rights Act in 1957.

Rosa Parks's courage reminds us all that the age and size of a person do not matter when he or she has something to say, something to believe in. A determined voice shall be heard.

ROSA PARKS, A WOMAN OF COURAGE—KUJICHAGULIA

A Story by Eloise Greenfield

Illustration by Carole Byard

On Thursday evening, December 1, 1955, Mrs. Parks left work and started home. She was tired. Her shoulders ached from bending over the sewing machine all day. "Today, I'll ride the bus," she thought.

She got on and sat in the first seat for blacks, right behind the white section. After a few stops the seats were filled. A white man got on. He looked for an empty seat. Then he looked at the driver. The driver came over to Mrs. Parks.

"You have to get up," he said.

All of a sudden Rosa Parks knew she was not going to give up her seat. It was not fair. She had paid her money just as the man had. This time she was not going to move.

"No," she said softly.

"You'd better get up or I'll call the police," the driver said.

It was very quiet on the bus now. Everyone stopped talking and watched. Still, Rosa Parks did not move.

"Are you going to get up?"

"No," she repeated.

The driver left the bus and returned with two policemen. "You're under arrest," they told her.

Mrs. Parks walked off the bus. The policemen put her in their car and drove to the police station. One policeman stuck a camera in her face and took her picture. Another took her fingerprints. Then she was locked in a cell.

Mrs. Parks felt very bad, sitting in that little room with iron bars. But she did not cry. She was a religious woman, and she thought of her faith in God. She said a silent prayer. Then she waited.

Someone who had seen Rosa Parks arrested called Edgar Daniel Nixon of the NAACP. Mr. Nixon went right away to the police station and posted a hundred-dollar bond for Mrs. Parks. This meant that she could leave but that she promised to go to court on Monday for her trial.

Mrs. Parks left the police station. She had been locked up for two and a half hours. Mr. Nixon drove her home. At her apartment Mrs. Parks, her husband, Mr. Nixon, and Fred Gray, a lawyer, talked about what had happened. They thought they saw a way to solve the problem of the buses.

Mr. Gray would go into court with Mrs. Parks. He would prove that the bus company was not obeying the United States Constitution. The Constitution is an important paper that was written by the men who started the United States. It says that all the citizens of the United States must be treated fairly.

The next morning Rosa Parks went to her job as usual. Her employer was surprised to see her. He had read about her arrest in the newspaper, and he thought she would be too upset to come in. Some of the white workers gave Mrs. Parks mean looks and would not speak to her. But she went on with her work.

That night Mrs. Parks met with a group of ministers and other black leaders of the city. Dr. Martin Luther King, Jr., was one of the ministers. The black men and women of Montgomery were angry again. But this time they knew what to do.

"If the bus company won't treat us courteously," one leader said, "we won't spend our money to ride the buses. We'll walk!"

After that meeting some of the people printed little sheets of paper. These sheets of paper, called leaflets, said: DON'T RIDE THE BUS TO WORK, TO TOWN, TO SCHOOL, OR ANYWHERE, MONDAY, DECEMBER 5. They also invited people to a church meeting on Monday night. The leaflets were left everywhere—in mailboxes, on porches, in drugstores.

On Sunday morning black ministers all over the city preached about Rosa Parks in their churches. Dr. King preached from his pulpit at the Dexter Avenue Baptist Church.

The preachers said, "Brothers and sisters, if you don't like what happened to Rosa Parks and what has been happening to us all these years, do something about it. Walk!"

And the people said, "Amen. We'll walk."

On Monday morning, no one was riding the buses. There were many people on the street, but everyone was walking. They were cheering because the buses were empty.

Rosa Parks got up early that morning. She went to court with her lawyer for her trial. The judge found her guilty. But she and her lawyer did not agree with him. Her lawyer said, "We'll get a higher court to decide. If we have to, we'll take the case to the highest court in the United States."

1955

Montgomery City LINES BUS Company

That night thousands of people went to the church meeting. There were so many people that most of them had to stand outside and listen through a loudspeaker.

First there was prayer. Then Rosa Parks was introduced. She stood up slowly. The audience rose to its feet and clapped and cheered. After Mrs. Parks sat down, several ministers gave their speeches. Finally Dr. Martin Luther King started to speak.

"We are tired," he said.

"Yes, Lord," the crowd answered.

"We're not going to be kicked around anymore," Dr. King said. "We walked one day. Now we are going to have a real protest. We are going to keep walking until the bus company gives us fair treatment."

After Dr. King finished speaking, the Montgomery Improvement Association was formed to plan the protest. Dr. King was made president.

Then there was hymn singing and hand clapping. The people went home feeling good. All that walking was not going to be easy, but they knew they could do it.

The Montgomery Improvement Association and the churches bought as many cars and station wagons as they could afford. There were telephone numbers that people could call when they needed a ride. Women who worked at home answered the phones. Rosa Parks was one of them. Her employer had told her that she was no longer needed. When someone called for a ride, Mrs. Parks would tell the drivers where to go. But there were not nearly enough cars.

Old people and young people walked. The children walked a long way to school. The men and women walked to work, to church, everywhere. In the morning it was like a parade. People were going to work, some riding on the backs of mules, some riding in wagons pulled by horses, but most of them walking. Sometimes they sang.

In the evening the parade went the other way, people going home. The newspapers called Montgomery "the walking city."

Rosa Parks began to travel to other cities, making speeches. She told about the hardships of the people. Many of the people she spoke to helped. They gave her money to pay for bonds and to buy gas for cars.

The black citizens of Montgomery walked all winter, all spring, all summer and fall in all kinds of weather. The bus company lost thousands of dollars.

In November, the Supreme Court, the highest court in the United States, said that the bus company had to change.

THIRD DAY

Green candle
December 28, third day of Kwanzaa
Principle: Ujima (collective work and responsibility)
Symbol: Kinara (wooden candle holder)

Come together! Come together! We must catch Sungura the Rabbit. We must keep him away from the water hole. You see, Sungura loves to drink water, but he doesn't want to help dig for it. He lives in East Africa, where a season can be long and dry. We will have to use Ujima in order to catch him. In other words, I need you to help me tell the story.

Let us travel to Kenya, a beautiful country in East Africa. Kenya is the place where Sungura lives. Let us create a magical forest.

STORYTELLER*

I am the tall mango tree.

GATHERING

I am the tall mango tree.

STORYTELLER *(mimes the action)*

Raise your hands up high. Wave your leaves. Shake your fruits—SHAY-SHAYSHAYSHAY!

GATHERING *(waves and shakes hands)*

SHAYSHAYSHAYSHAY!

STORYTELLER *(mimes the action)*

I am the river.

*Note: The storyteller may have a story bag with pieces of cloth, bells, and other objects in it in order to enhance the telling of the story. The storyteller should also use hands, body, and face to mimic creatures and places to set the scene of the story.

Floowing! Floowing!

GATHERING

I am the river.

Floowing! Floowing!

STORYTELLER *(lifts hands to face and cups hands underneath, putting on a beautiful smile)*

I am the sun laughing.

HA! HA! HA! HA! HA!

GATHERING

I am the sun laughing.

HA! HA! HA! HA! HA!

STORYTELLER *(raising arms and hands into a triangle-shaped mountain)*

I am the mountain high.

GATHERING

I am the mountain high.

STORYTELLER *(mimes the action)*

I am the coool breeze.

(loud) Bloooowing! *(louder)* Bloooowing!

GATHERING

I am the coool breeze.

Bloooowing! Bloooowing!

STORYTELLER *(wiggles fingers)*

I am the stars.

Twinkling! Twinkling!

GATHERING

I am the stars.

Twinkling! Twinkling!

STORYTELLER

I am the storyteller, ready to begin.

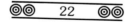

I am the storyteller, ready to begin.

The tone has been set; the gathering is ready. The storyteller begins the story.

RABBIT AT THE WATER HOLE—UJIMA
Illustration by Leo and Diane Dillon

STORYTELLER

There was once a time in the forest when a very strange thing happened: All the rain just stopped raining. All the rivers just stopped flowing. And all the land dried up. There was no water. The animals were very thirsty. They became frightened. They moaned and groaned. Ooooah! Ooooah!

GATHERING

Ooooah! Ooooah!

STORYTELLER

They walk, walk, walk, walk, walk. And they talk, talk, talk, talk, talk. The elephant sounds his trumpet, Truuuump!

GATHERING

Truuuump!

STORYTELLER

The gorilla beat his drum, Bumbumbumbum. Bumbumbumbum.

GATHERING

Bumbumbumbum.

STORYTELLER

And then, suddenly, out of the bush came the lion, GRRROOOWL! (Storyteller becomes the lion by staring intently at the audience and pacing about. In the lion's voice:)

"Our water hole has dried up. What are we going to do about it? Who has an idea?"

A little bitty timid chipmunk raised his hand and said,

"Lion, Lion. Let's dig a water hole. Let's dig into the ground."

"An excellent idea,"

said the lion.

"Thank you, little chipmunk."

All of the animals agreed to dig for water except Sungura the Rabbit.

"I'm too tired to dig for water."

Sungura the Rabbit hopped away.

Hippity hoppity.

Hippity hoppity. Hippity hoppity.

"Grrroowl,"

said the lion.

"We'll deal with Sungura the Rabbit later.

We must cooperate. We must work together.

Get your shovels and let's dig for water."

(Storyteller asks gathering to join in)

GATHERING

Heeave ho-ho. Heeave ho-ho.

Dig Dig Dig Dig Dig Dig Dig

STORYTELLER *(as the lion)*

"Wait a minute. I think I've found something.

It's cool. It's clear. It's fresh.

It's water. Save yourselves. Drink it.

Wash your hands in it. Throw some on your faces.

Everybody say Yaaaaaay!"

GATHERING

YAAAAAAAY!

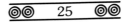

STORYTELLER

The water began to flow. The grasses began to grow. The night was so happy and all of the stars came back to the sky.

"It is true that we have our water back,"
said the lion,

"But did everyone help us dig for it?"

GATHERING

NO!

STORYTELLER

Who refused to help dig?

GATHERING

Sungura the Rabbit.

STORYTELLER

Should we give Sungura the Rabbit some of our water, or should we teach him a lesson?

GATHERING

Teach him a lesson.

STORYTELLER

Perhaps the water buffalo can keep him away from our water hole. Who wants to be the water buffalo? Raise your hands.
(Storyteller chooses a volunteer from the gathering)
Water Buffalo, your sound is something like a cow or a bull. MOOOOO!
Use your imagination and let us hear your sound loud and clear.

WATER BUFFALO

MOOOOOO!

STORYTELLER

That's wonderful. The water hole is right in front of you, Water Buffalo. Drink some.
(Water buffalo drinks water)

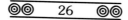

Stay here. Sungura the Rabbit will be coming soon. Later that night, when all the stars were twinkling brightly, that tricky Sungura the Rabbit came hopping up.

STORYTELLER *(as Sungura)*

"Hey, Water Buffalo, how ya doing? You looking good. I got a present for you. Put your hands together. I have brought you some honey! Go ahead, eat it. That's right, eat it."

And while the water buffalo ate the honey, that tricky rabbit bent down, took some water, and hopped away.

STORYTELLER *(as Sungura)*

"HAHAHAHAHAHAHA!"

The next morning, the animals walked over to see the water buffalo. Water Buffalo, what have you been eating?

WATER BUFFALO

Honey!

STORYTELLER

Who gave you this honey?

WATER BUFFALO

Sungura the Rabbit.

STORYTELLER

Did Sungura get any water?

WATER BUFFALO

Yes, he did.

STORYTELLER

Oh, Noooooooo!

(Storyteller and group clap for the water buffalo, who returns to the gathering)

Who can keep Sungura away? Perhaps the hyena can. Raise your hand if you want to be the hyena.

(Storyteller chooses volunteer number two)

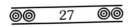

The hyena loves to laugh. HEEEEY! HEEEEEEY! Use your imagination, Hyena, and let us hear your giggles and laughs loud and clear.

HYENA

Heeeeeey! Heeeeeey!

STORYTELLER

That's great! The water hole is right in front of you, Hyena. Drink some. *(Hyena drinks water)*

Stay here. Sungura the Rabbit will be coming soon. Later that night, when all the stars were twinkling brightly, that tricky Sungura the Rabbit came hopping up.

STORYTELLER *(as Sungura)*

"Uh oh, that's the hyena. He thinks he's so slick. But wait until he sees my trick."

Sungura went over to the grasses. Blade by blade, he began weaving them together until he made a blanket.

Sishsishsishsishsishsish.

(Storyteller pulls a piece of green printed cloth from her bag. The cloth is African fabric with leaves)

He threw the blanket over his head and danced toward the hyena. Slowly, Sungura the Rabbit began wrapping the blanket of grass around and around and around the hyena, so the hyena couldn't move. The tricky rabbit bent down, took some water, and hopped away.

STORYTELLER *(as Sungura)*

"Siiiiiip! Siiiiip! Siiiiiip! HA! HA! HA! HA! HA!"

The next morning the animals walked over to see the hyena.

Who wrapped you in this blanket?

HYENA

Sungura the Rabbit.

STORYTELLER

Did Sungura get any water?

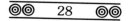

HYENA

Yes, I think so.

(Storyteller unwraps the hyena)

STORYTELLER

Oh Nooooo!

(Storyteller and group clap for the hyena, who returns to the gathering)

Who can keep Sungura away? Perhaps the turtle can.

Raise your hand if you want to be the turtle.

(Storyteller chooses volunteer number three)

What do turtles carry on their backs?

GATHERING

Their shell.

STORYTELLER

Turtle, let me make you a shell.

(Storyteller takes the green cloth that was wrapped around the hyena and drapes it across the turtle's back and shoulders. She ties the top and bottom ends of the cloth on the right side around the turtle's right arm. Then she ties the top and bottom ends of the cloth on the left side around the turtle's left arm, creating a pattern of a shell. She turns the turtle's back to the gathering so they can see the shell)

How does the turtle move, fast or slow?

TURTLE

Slow.

STORYTELLER

Use your imagination, Turtle, and walk slowly.

(The turtle moves slowly across the story circle)

Stop, Turtle, and look up high at that big beautiful tree in front of you. Wiggle your fingers and take some sap from the tree. Rub the sap on your back.

(Storyteller helps put sap on the turtle's shell)

OK, Turtle, let's walk over to the water hole.

(Storyteller directs the turtle to the water hole)

Drink some water, Turtle.

(Turtle drinks the water)

Bend down into the water, Turtle. Stick your head inside your shell and fold your arms. Don't move, Turtle. I hear Sungura the Rabbit.

STORYTELLER *(as Sungura)*

Hippity hoppity hippity hoppity. "Ha! Ha! Ha!"

(looking around)

"There's nobody here. The water is all mine. There's even a shiny stone I can sit on."

But when Sungura the Rabbit bent down to touch the smooth stone, his hands became stuck. Because the smooth stone was—

GATHERING

The turtle's shell.

STORYTELLER

And what was on the turtle's back?

GATHERING

Sap.

STORYTELLER

And sap is very what?

GATHERING

Sticky.

STORYTELLER *(as Sungura)*

"Heeeelp! Help! Heeeelp! Let me go."

The turtle stood up in the water and said in a loud, proud voice, "I caught Sungura the Rabbit!"

TURTLE

I caught Sungura the Rabbit!

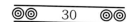

STORYTELLER

Let's clap for the turtle.

GATHERING *(claps)*

STORYTELLER

We hope Sungura will remember *(motions for gathering to repeat after her)* NO WORK! NO WATER!

GATHERING

NO WORK! NO WATER!

Red candle
December 29, fourth day of Kwanzaa
Principle: Ujamaa (cooperative economics)
Symbol: Muhindi (ears of corn)

▼

In Accra, Ghana, the marketplace is a bustling, busy place. Rows of tables filled with cassava, mangoes, tomatoes, yams, and hot peppers line the streets. A maze of market stalls display baskets, pots, cloths, and jewelry. Children carrying trays of baked goods on their heads mingle through swarms of people. Farmers, herdsmen, traders, and craftspeople busily sell and exchange their wares. Singers, flute players, and drummers delight the crowds by making musical sounds.

A person can always bargain for a ''suitable'' price and one never leaves empty handed. Everyone cooperates in the marketplace for the greater whole like spokes on a wheel. That is why Tortoise goes to the marketplace to join the greater community. As the saying goes, Tortoise moves slowly but he always reaches the marketplace.

A DAY IN THE MARKETPLACE—UJAMAA

Illustration by Jerry Pinkney

One day Tortoise went to the marketplace to buy sweet potatoes from the sweet potato man. Tortoise loved sweet potatoes. He bought as many as he could carry. The sweet potato man put them in a large sack. Tortoise threw the heavy sack of sweet potatoes over his back. Walking through the marketplace, he headed for home singing a little song:

"Sweet potato, very sweet,
Sweet potato, good to eat.

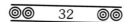

Sweet potato, hum hum,
Sweet potato, yum yum.''

While tortoise was walking, the weighty sweet potatoes ripped a hole in the sack. The hole grew bigger, and one by one the sweet potatoes fell to the ground.

A goat saw them and ate all of them. When Tortoise turned around and saw what the goat had done, he became upset and said,

"Sweet Potato Man gave me sweet potatoes
for my hard-earned money,
but you, Goat, ate all my sweet potatoes.
AND SO NOW I WILL EAT YOU.''

But the goatherd cried out,

"Please, Tortoise, don't eat my goat. She's all I've got.
Let me give you some of her fresh milk.''

Tortoise agreed to take the milk. The goatherd poured the milk into a calabash. Tortoise put the calabash on top of his head and continued walking through the marketplace. High above, on one of the market stalls, sat Fabric Lady's pet monkey. The monkey saw the milk and it made him very thirsty. He jumped down into the calabash and drank all of it. Tortoise became upset and said,

"Sweet Potato Man gave me sweet potatoes
for my hard-earned money,
but the goat ate all my sweet potatoes.
The goatherd gave me fresh milk
so I wouldn't eat the goat,
but you, Monkey, drank all my fresh milk.
AND SO NOW I WILL EAT YOU!''

The fabric lady cried out,

"Please, Tortoise, don't eat my monkey.
My pet is my dear friend. Let me give you
a piece of my beautiful cloth."

Tortoise agreed to take the cloth. The fabric lady gave him a piece of cloth designed with bright red and yellow flowers. Tortoise draped the cloth across his shoulders. He strolled proudly through the marketplace.

The honey gatherers' bees saw Tortoise's cloth. They thought the flowers were real. They buzzed around Tortoise stinging his shoulders and tearing the cloth. Tortoise became very upset and said,

"Sweet Potato Man gave me sweet potatoes
for my hard-earned money,
but the goat ate all my sweet potatoes.
The goatherd gave me fresh milk
so I wouldn't eat the goat,
but the pet monkey drank all my fresh milk.
The fabric lady gave me pretty cloth
so I wouldn't eat the pet monkey,
but you, Bees, tore my pretty cloth.
AND SO NOW I WILL EAT YOU."

The honey gatherers cried out,

"Please, Tortoise, don't take our bees.
They make tasty honey. We will give you
a pot full of it."

Tortoise agreed to take the pot of honey. He tied the pot around his waist. Tortoise continued walking through the marketplace. He passed by the egg man's stall as he was feeding seeds to his chickens. Some of the seeds scattered around Tortoise's feet. The chickens ran in front of him. Tortoise fell down and rolled this way and that way into the seeds. He was covered from head to toe with dusty honey and seeds. The chickens pecked at him, causing

him and the pot to roll into the river. When Tortoise swam out of the river, his
honey was all gone. He was very upset and he said,

"Sweet Potato Man gave me sweet potatoes
for my hard-earned money,
but the goat ate all my sweet potatoes.
The goatherd gave me fresh milk
so I wouldn't eat the goat,
but the pet monkey drank all my fresh milk.
The fabric lady gave me pretty cloth
so I wouldn't eat the pet monkey,
but the honeybees tore my pretty cloth.
The honey gatherers gave me tasty honey
so I wouldn't eat the honeybees,
but you, Chickens, threw my tasty honey
into the river.
AND SO NOW I WILL EAT YOU."

The egg man cried out,

"Please, Tortoise, don't eat my chickens.
I will give you three brown eggs."

Tortoise agreed to take the eggs. He placed them carefully inside his
shell and continued walking through the marketplace. He passed by a stall
containing baskets of all sizes and shapes. An egg snake slithered from one of
the baskets. The egg snake loved eggs as much as Tortoise loved sweet
potatoes. He crawled up into Tortoise's shell and began tickling him. While
Tortoise laughed loudly,

"Hee hee hee, hee hee hee,"

the egg snake swallowed each egg whole. Then he spat out the shells. The egg
snake loved eggs but he didn't like the shells.

Even though Tortoise was mad, he couldn't stop laughing. Finally the egg snake crawled out from under Tortoise's shell. Tortoise was very, very upset, and he said,

"Sweet Potato Man gave me sweet potatoes
for my hard-earned money,
but the goat ate all my sweet potatoes.
The goatherd gave me fresh milk
so I wouldn't eat the goat,
but the pet monkey drank all my fresh milk.
The fabric lady gave me pretty cloth
so I wouldn't eat the pet monkey,
but the honeybees tore my pretty cloth.
The honey gatherers gave me tasty honey
so I wouldn't eat the honeybees,
but the chickens threw my tasty honey
into the river.
The egg man gave me three brown eggs
so I wouldn't eat the chickens,
but you, Egg Snake, have swallowed my
three eggs.
AND SO NOW I WILL EAT YOU."

The basketweaver cried out,

"Please, Tortoise, don't eat my egg snake.
I will give you six straw baskets."

Tortoise agreed to take the baskets. He hurried through the marketplace as fast as his slow legs could carry him. The sweet potato man saw him and yelled,

"Hey, Tortoise, may I see your baskets?"

Tortoise was very upset. He jumped up and down and said,

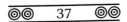

"You, Sweet Potato Man, gave me sweet potatoes
for my hard-earned money,
but the goat ate all my sweet potatoes.
The goatherd gave me fresh milk
so I wouldn't eat the goat,
but the pet monkey drank all my fresh milk.
The fabric lady gave me pretty cloth
so I wouldn't eat the pet monkey,
but the honeybees tore my pretty cloth.
The honey gatherers gave me tasty honey
so I wouldn't eat the honeybees,
but the chickens threw my tasty honey
into the river.
The egg man gave me three brown eggs
so I wouldn't eat the chickens,
but the egg snake ate my three brown eggs.
The basketweaver gave me six straw baskets
so I wouldn't eat the egg snake,
and so now you, Sweet Potato Man, want to
take my baskets?"

"Oh yes,"

said the sweet potato man.

"I can put my sweet potatoes in them.
Tortoise, I will give you twelve of my
finest sweets if you give me your six
straw baskets."

Tortoise cheerfully agreed to take the sweet potatoes. He went home
and baked a big sweet-potato pie.

"What a fantastic day I had at the marketplace,"

said Tortoise, as he ate a slice of pie.

"And if it had not been for
the basketweaver and her egg snake,
the egg man and his chickens,
the honey gatherers and their honeybees,
the fabric lady and her pet monkey,
and the goatherd and his goat,
the sweet potato man would not have given me
twelve of his finest sweet potatoes
to make this sweet-potato pie."

Tortoise went back to the marketplace and shared the sweet-potato pie with all of them. The sweet potato man, the goatherd, the fabric lady, the honey gatherers, the egg man, the basketweaver, and Tortoise gleefully sang a little song:

"Sweet potato, very sweet,
Sweet potato, good to eat.
Sweet potato, hum hum,
Sweet potato, yum yum."

FIFTH DAY

Green candle
December 30, fifth day of Kwanzaa
Principle: Nia (purpose)
Symbol: Zawadi (handmade gift or book)

Bredda Anancy, the trickster spider, always has a purpose in mind. In the Caribbean and in Latin America, the people tell tall stories about Bredda Anancy. Some say he is a spider. Some say he is an old man. Everyone says he is clever and uses his wit to get in and out of sticky situations. Bredda Anancy came from West Africa, where he was known as "Anansi." He traveled on the slave ship to the Americas. He is very popular because, right or wrong, he always has a way to solve his problems. A master drummer from Ghana once told me, "Spider stories are funny, this is true. But their meanings are a very serious matter."

Having a purpose in life helps you achieve many goals. Your plans may not always go in the direction you want them to go. Sometimes plans have to be changed in the middle of things. But any plan is better than no plan. Bredda Anancy always has a plan.

BREDDA ANANCY AND HIS COMMON SENSE—NIA
Illustration by Jonathan Green

Bredda Anancy is always full of ideas. One morning he woke up with a great idea in his head. "I will have a party," he said. "I will invite all me friends. They will bring lots of food. And I will be able to eat, eat, eat, eat, eat," which is what Bredda Anancy liked to do best.

Spinning his web, Bredda Anancy went to visit his friend Bredda Monkey. Knock! Knock! Bredda Anancy pounded on Bredda Monkey's tree house.

Bredda Monkey did not want anyone banging on his door so early in the morning, so he said, "GWAN, MON, whoever you are, before you shake me coconuts loose from me tree house. GWAN, MON!"

"That is not such a bad idea," thought Bredda Anancy. So he knocked even harder until a coconut fell right into his web. "Hmmmm, nothing tastes better than fresh coconut water," laughed Bredda Anancy. He yelled at Bredda Monkey, "Your coconut water tastes very ire this morning, Mon. Hey, Mon, you hear me, eh?"

Bredda Monkey was angry. "You who bangs on me door, you who wakes me up, you who drinks from me coconut, who are you, Mon?"

"If you stick your head out the window," said Anancy, "you will realize that it is your good friend Bredda Anancy."

Bredda Monkey knew that Bredda Anancy probably had a trick or two up his sleeve, but he was curious, so he stuck his head out his window and said, "Good mawnin, me dear Bredda Anancy. What's up, Mon?"

"Good mawnin, Mon," said Anancy. "I have something to tell you, Mon." Bredda Monkey swung down from his tree. "How are you feeling today, Bredda Monkey?" asked Bredda Anancy.

"I don't know yet," answered Bredda Monkey. "Ask me again after you tell me what you want, Mon."

Bredda Anancy and Bredda Monkey were very good friends, even though Bredda Anancy was always tricking Bredda Monkey into doing something he did not want to do. But Bredda Monkey could never figure a way to say no.

"Bredda Monkey," said Anancy, "I want you to be the first to know that I'm having a party tonight."

Bredda Monkey loved parties. "Thank you, Bredda Anancy. I'm honored that you have told me first."

"I'm glad you feel this way. Therefore, you will help me, yes?" said Bredda Anancy.

"Oh yes," said Bredda Monkey. "Wha yu wan me do, Mon?"

"I want you to tell all our friends to come."

"Yes, I will tell some and you will tell some, no?" asked Bredda Monkey.

"Oh no," said Bredda Anancy. "I have honored you by telling you. The party is me idea. The least you could do is tell all the others," said Bredda Anancy.

"Very well," said Bredda Monkey.

"Tell them to bring food," said Bredda Anancy. "Tell some to bring rice and peas, some to bring carrot juice, some to bring Johnny cakes and plantains, and you, Bredda Monkey, may bring coconuts and bananas."

"And what will you bring?" asked Bredda Monkey.

"I don't have to bring anything; after all, the party is being held at me house," answered Bredda Anancy.

"Very well," said Bredda Monkey. "I will tell everyone except Señor Tiger. He should not come."

"And why not?" asked Bredda Anancy. "Señor Tiger has a big appetite, and he will bring lots of food, Mon."

"That's what worries me—Señor Tiger's appetite. He might get carried away and eat everybody," said Bredda Monkey.

"That's nonsense," said Bredda Anancy. "Me common sense tells me that we should invite him, Mon."

"Well, me common sense says that we should *not* invite him, and I have more common sense than you," Bredda Monkey said as he jumped up and down. He pranced around and around. "I got common sense all over me body. In me feet, me back, me elbows, me hips, and me neck, Mon."

Bredda Anancy noticed that Bredda Monkey didn't mention whether or not he had any sense in his head. Bredda Anancy didn't have time to argue. So he said, "Me dear Bredda Monkey, I just got a little bit of common sense in me head. I use a little bit for me and I'll use a little bit for you, because you are me dear friend."

"Well, thank you," said Bredda Monkey as he climbed up to his tree house. He began swinging from branch to branch, telling the animals about Bredda Anancy's party. Meanwhile, Bredda Anancy went home to prepare for the party. "Me common sense tells me to think of a plan if Bredda Monkey doesn't invite Señor Tiger to the party."

When Bredda Monkey came to Señor Tiger's house, he peeped in and saw that Señor Tiger was taking a nap. So he whispered quietly, "Señor Tiger, you are invited to Bredda Anancy's party tonight." Then Bredda Monkey scurried away.

Later that evening, the party guests strolled to Bredda Anancy's house. Bredda Monkey was the first one to arrive. He strolled in laughing louder than anyone. John Crow escorted Nanny Goat. Compere Rabbit hopped in with Mrs. Rabbit. Sis Cow came in with Old Bull. Compere Donkey brayed as he entered. The Hummingbirds flew in from Haiti. Bredda Snake and his steel band came in from Trinidad. Bredda Alligator, Bredda Rat, and Bredda Dog sang calypso and reggae songs.

"Where is Señor Tiger?" asked Bredda Anancy. "Did you tell him about me party, Mon?"

Bredda Monkey stopped laughing. "Yes, I-I-I told him," said Bredda Monkey hesitantly. "But I-I-I don't think he is coming."

"And why not?" asked Bredda Anancy. "Wha he say, Mon?"

"He was napping when I told him," replied Bredda Monkey.

"Common sense told me to have a plan in the back of me mind," said Bredda Anancy. "I think you should be prepared also, Bredda Monkey."

"Me dear friend, forget about your common sense. Stop worrying," said Bredda Monkey. "Drink some carrot juice, Mon."

There was much to worry about. Señor Tiger could hear the music. "Someone is having a party without me," he said. "Who insults me this way?" His ears led him in the direction the sweet sounds were coming from. He stuck his head in Bredda Anancy's window and yelled, *"¡Hola!* How dare you, Bredda Anancy!" Señor Tiger growled, "GRRRRooOWL!" The party guests scurried away like ants. Bredda Monkey ran faster than anyone. He jumped into his tree house and pulled down all the shades. Señor Tiger grabbed Bredda Anancy.

"Wait, Señor Tiger. Please listen to me," pleaded Bredda Anancy. "I told Bredda Monkey to tell everyone to come. He told you while you were taking a nap."

Señor Tiger ran to Bredda Monkey's tree house. He shook the trunk of the house with all of his strength. Coconuts went flying everywhere. Bredda Monkey latched onto a limb and swung over to Bredda Anancy's house.

"Help! Help me, Bredda Anancy!" screamed Bredda Monkey. "Señor Tiger is after me."

"Use your common sense. Remember, you have more than me do, Mon," said Bredda Anancy.

"I don't have time, Mon. He is coming," pleaded Bredda Monkey.

"Do you know any riddles?" asked Bredda Anancy.

"How can you joke at a time like this?" asked Bredda Monkey.

Bredda Anancy finally convinced Bredda Monkey to think of some riddles. Bredda Monkey began talking:

> "Riddle me this, Riddle me that,
> Guess me riddle, Or perhaps not."

Señor Tiger bolted through the door. Bredda Anancy fell down on the ground. He rolled from side to side, pretending he was laughing.

"Ho ho ho, Bredda Monkey. That's very ire, Mon," laughed Bredda Anancy.

"¿Qué pasa?" asked Señor Tiger.

Bredda Anancy tried to stand up. "Bredda Monkey tells the best riddles in the world."

Señor Tiger liked riddles. He asked Bredda Monkey to tell him a funny one.

Bredda Monkey nervously began talking.

> "Riddle me this, Riddle me that,
> Guess me riddle, Or perhaps not.
> Why did the rooster walk across the road?"

"I've heard this one before," said Señor Tiger. "To get to the other side."

"No," said Bredda Monkey. "The rooster walked across because he didn't have a bicycle."

"Ha Ha Ha!" Señor Tiger laughed. *"Sí, sí. That is very good, amigo."*

Bredda Monkey told riddles for the next hour. Señor Tiger soon forgot about why he was angry with Bredda Monkey.

"I think you have found a purpose in life, Bredda Monkey," said Señor Tiger.

"Oh. What's that?" asked Bredda Monkey.

"To tell me riddles, of course," said Señor Tiger. "I will visit you *every* morning, and I want you to have a riddle waiting for me. *Adiós, amigos.*"

Señor Tiger went home. Bredda Monkey didn't want Señor Tiger coming to his house every morning, but he was too afraid to do anything about it.

"What a purpose in life I have," Bredda Monkey said sadly.

"I told you to use your common sense," said Bredda Anancy. "As for me, that is me sole purpose in life—to use me common sense for me and save a little bit for me friend."

Gwan, Mon—Go away, Man
Mon—Man
Me—I, my
Good mawnin—Good morning
Ire *(i-ree)*—good
Wha yu wan me do, Mon?—What do you want me to do, Man?
Wha me say?—What did I say?
Bredda—Brother

Señor, Compere—Mr.
Hola (o-lah)—Hi
Qué pasa—What's happening?
Sí—Yes
Adiós, amigos—Goodbye, friends

Red candle
December 31, sixth day of Kwanzaa
Principle: Kuumba (creativity)
Symbol: Kikombe Cha Umoja (unity cup)

My grandaddy used to say, "Honey child, you got the power to make something beautiful in this world. We all do. But when we can't share our creative energy, it makes us mighty frustrated." Then he would capture my imagination by telling me one of his favorite tales so I could understand what he was talking about. It was about this little animal that had lots of Kuumba, creativity.

THE FROG WHO WANTED TO BE A SINGER—KUUMBA
A Boogie-Woogie Tale
Illustration by Floyd Cooper

Friends, let's go back. Back to the forest. Back to the motherland. Back to the days when the animals talked and walked upon the earth as folks do now.

Let's examine a little creature who is feeling mighty bad, mighty sad, mighty frustrated. We call him the frog. There's nothing wrong in being a frog. But this particular frog feels that he has talent. You see, he wants to be a singer. And there's nothing wrong in wanting to be a singer except that in this particular forest where this particular frog lives, frogs don't sing. Only the birds are allowed to sing. The birds are considered the most beautiful singers in the forest.

So, for a while, the frog is cool. He's quiet. He stays to himself and practices on his lily pad, jumping up and down, singing to himself. But one day all of this frustration begins to swell inside him. He becomes so swollen that frustration bubbles start popping from his mouth, his ears, his nose, even from his eyes, and he says to himself (in a froglike voice): "You know, I'm tired of feeling this way. I'm tired of holding all this inside me. I've got talent. I want to be a singer."

The little frog decides to share his ambitions with his parents. His parents are somewhat worried about his desires, but since he is their son, they encourage him and say, "Son, we're behind you one hundred percent. If that's what you want to be, then go right ahead. You'll make us very proud."

This makes the frog feel better. It gives him some confidence, so much so that he decides to share the good news with his friends. He jumps over to the other side of the pond and says, "Fellows, I want to share something with you."

"Good!" they reply. "You got some flies we can eat?"

"No, not flies. I got talent. I want to be a singer."

"Fool, are you crazy?" says one friend. "Frogs don't sing in this place. You'd better keep your big mouth shut."

They laugh at the frog, so he jumps back over to his lily pad. He rocks back and forth, meditating and contemplating his situation, and begins to realize that perhaps he should go and talk with the birds. They seem reasonable enough; maybe they will allow him to join their singing group.

He gathers up his confidence, jumps over to their tree house, and knocks on their trunk. The head bird flies to the window, looks down on the frog's head, and says, "Oh, it's the frog. How may we help you?"

"Can I come up? I got something to ask you," says the frog.

"Very well, Frog. Do jump up."

Frog enters the tree house, and hundreds of birds begin fluttering around him.

"Come on in, Frog. Why don't you sit over there in the corner," says the head bird. Frog sits down, but he feels a little shy. He begins to chew on his tongue.

"Frog, how may we help you?"

"Uh, well, uh, you see," says Frog, "I would like to become a part of your group."

"That's wonderful," says the head bird.

"Yes, wonderful," echo the other birds.

"Frog, you may help us carry our worms," said the head bird.

"That's not what I had in mind," says Frog.

"Well, what do you have in mind?"

Frog begins to stutter. "I-I-I-I want to-to-to sing wi-wi-with your group."

"What! You must be joking, of course. An ugly green frog who is full of warts sing with us delicate creatures? You would cause us great embarrassment."

"B-b-but . . ." Frog tries to plead his case, but the head bird becomes angry.

"Out! Out! Out of our house you go." He kicks the frog from the house. Frog rolls like a ball down the jungle path.

When he returns home, he feels very sad. The frog wants to cry but doesn't, even though he aches deep inside his gut. He wants to give up, but he doesn't. Instead he practices and practices and practices.

Then he begins to think again and realizes that even though the birds sing every Friday night at the Big Time Weekly Concert, they don't control it. The fox is in charge. The frog jumps over to the fox's place and knocks on his cave.

"Brother Fox, Brother Fox, it's me, Frog. I want to talk to you."

The fox is a fast talker and a busy worker, and really doesn't want to be bothered with the frog.

"Quick, quick, what do you want to do?"

"I want to sing," says the frog.

"Sing? Get out of here, quick, quick, quick!"

"Please, Brother Fox. Please give me a chance."

"Hmmmm," says the fox, shifting his eyes. "Uh, you know something, Froggie? Maybe I could use you. Why don't you show up Friday, at eight o'clock sharp, okay?"

"You mean I can do it?"

"That's what I said. Now get out of here. Quick, quick, quick!"

Oh, the frog is happy. He is going to "do his thing." He is going to present himself to the world.

Meanwhile, the fox goes around to the animals in the forest and tells them about the frog's plans. Each animal promises to be there and give the frog a "little present" for his singing debut.

And so Monday rolls around, Tuesday rolls around, Wednesday rolls around, Thursday rolls around, and it is Friday. The frog is so excited he bathes all day. He polishes his little green head. He scrubs his little green fingers and his little green toes. He looks at his little green reflection in the pond, smiles, and says, "Um, um, um, I am beauuuutiful! And I am going to 'do my thing' tonight." And soon it is seven o'clock, and then it is seven-thirty, and then it is seven forty-five, and there is the frog trembling, holding onto the edge of the curtain.

He looks out at the audience and sees all the animals gathering in their seats. The frog is scared, so scared that his legs won't stop trembling and his eyes won't stop twitching. Brother Fox strolls out onstage and the show begins.

"Thank you, thank you, thank you. Ladies and gentlemen, we have a wonderful show for you tonight. Presenting, for your entertainment, the frog who thinks he's a singer. Come on, let's clap. Come on out here, Frog, come on, come on. Let's give him a big hand." The animals clap and roar with laughter. The frog jumps out and slowly goes up to the microphone.

"For-for-for-for-for my first number, I-I-I-I—"

Now, before that frog can put the period at the end of that sentence, the elephant stands up, pulls down a pineapple, and throws it right at the frog's head.

"Ow!" cries the frog. And the lion pulls down a babab, throws it, and hits that frog right in the mouth. "Oh," gulps the frog. Other animals join in the act of throwing things at the frog. Some of them shout and yell at him, "Boo! Boo! Get off the stage. You stink! You're ugly. We don't want to hear a frog sing. Boo, you jive turkey!"

The poor little frog has to leap off the stage and run for his life. He hides underneath the stage. Brother Fox rushes back on the stage.

"Okay, okay, okay, calm down—just trying out our comic routine. We have some real talent for your enjoyment. Presenting the birds, who really can sing. Let's hear it for the birds." The audience claps loudly. The birds fly onto the stage, their heads held up high. Their wings slowly strike a stiff, hypnotic pose, as if they are statues. Their stage presence demands great respect from the audience. They chirp, tweet, and whistle, causing the audience to fall into a soft, peaceful nod.

Everyone is resting quietly except the frog, who is tired of being pushed around. The frog is tired of feeling frustrated. He leaps over the fox. He grabs him, shakes him, puts his hands around the fox's throat, and says, "You tried to make a fool out of me."

"Leave me alone," says the fox. "If you want to go back out there and make a fool of yourself, go right ahead."

"Hmph," says the frog. "That's just what I'm going to do." Now that little green frog hippity-hops back onto the stage. He is shaking but determined to sing his song.

"I don't care if you are asleep. I'm gonna wake you up. I came here to sing a song tonight, and that's what I'm going to do." In the style of what we call boogie-woogie, the frog begins to "do his thing":

DOOBA DOOBA DOOBA DOOBA DOOBA DOOBA DOOBA DOOBA
DOOBA DOOBA DOOBA DOOBA DOOBA DOOBA DOOBA DOOBA

The frog bops his head about as though it were a jazzy saxophone. His fingers move as though they were playing a funky bass fiddle.

DOOBA DOOBA DOOBA DOOBA DOOBADEE DOOBADEE
DOOBADEE DOOBADEE
DOOBA DOOBA DOOBA DOOBA DOOBADEE DOOBADEE
DOOBADEE DOOBADEE
DOOBA DOOBA DOOBA DOOBA DOOBA DOOBA DOOBA DOOBA
DOOBA
DOOBA! DOOBA! DOOP-DEE DOOP! .... BLURRRRRP!

The elephant opens one eye. He roars, "Uuumphf!" He jumps from his seat. He flings his hips from side to side, doing a dance we now call the "bump." The lion is the next animal to jump up from his seat. He shouts, "I love it! I love it!" He shakes his body thisaway and thataway and every whichaway, doing a dance we now call the "twist." Soon the snakes are boogalooing and the giraffes are doing the "jerk." The hyenas do the "slop" and the fox does the "mashed potato." The birds also want to join in: "We want to do Dooba Dooba, too." They chirp and sway through the trees.

Tweet Tweet Tweet Dooba
Tweet Tweet Tweet Dooba

The whole forest is rocking. The joint is jumping. The animals are snapping their fingers. They are dancing, doing something that they have never done before.

The fox runs back on the stage, grabs the mike, and shouts, "Wow, Frog, you are a genius. You have given us something new."

From then on, the frog is allowed to sing every Friday night at the Big Time Weekly Concert.

And, as my grandaddy used to say, that is how rhythm and blues was born.

DOOBA DOOBA DOOBA DOOBA DOOBA DOOBA DOOBA DOOBA
DOOBA! DOOBA! DOOP-DEE DOOP! . . . BLURRRRRP!

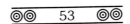

SEVENTH DAY

Green candle
January 1, seventh day of Kwanzaa
Principle: Imani (faith)
Symbol: Mishumaa Saba (seven candles)

▼

Imani means faith, so I've been told. So check out this rap for the young and the old. Keep Imani in your heart. Keep Imani in your soul. Imani is more precious than diamonds or gold.

KEEP THE FAITH, BABY—IMANI
Illustration by Jan Spivey Gilchrist

> Keep the faith, baby.
> That's the thing to do.
> Believe in yourself
> and your family too.
>
> Keep the faith, baby.
> That's the bottom line.
> If you really want to make it,
> then it's going to take time.
> It took 60 years
> and 600 miles
> for Clara Brown
> to find her slave child.
> It took guts and courage
> let the truth be told,
> for Harriet Tubman

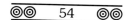

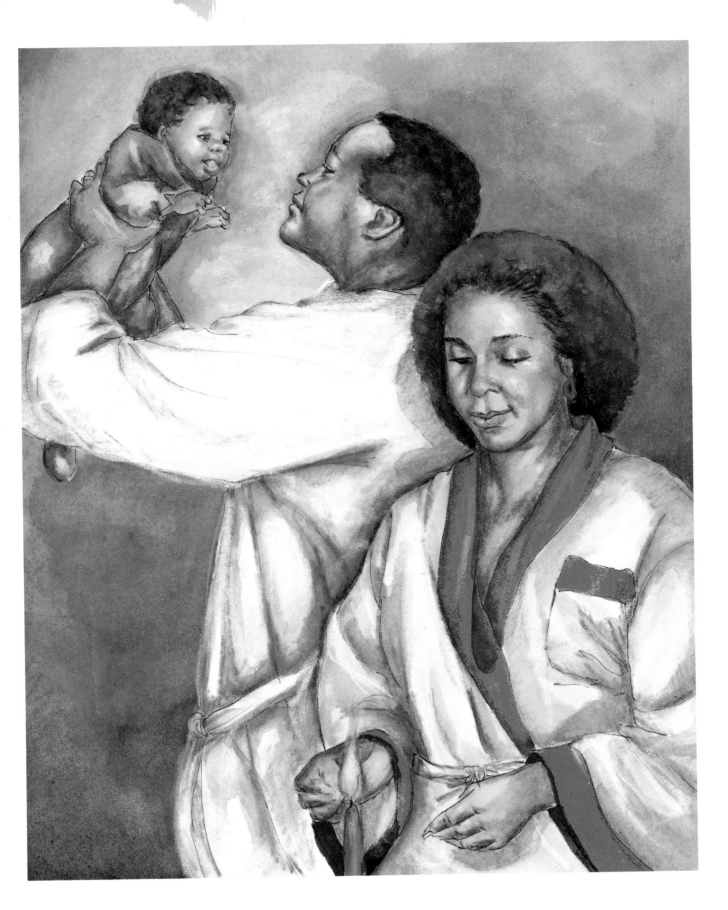

to work the Underground Railroad.
It took a lawyer named Marshall
and a little girl named Brown
for the Supreme Court
to strike school segregation down.
It took most of a lifetime
dedication and knowledge
for Mary McLeod Bethune
to build a college.
It took hours and hours
of hard work and pain
for Muhammad Ali
to be a champion, again.
It took 27 years
but he still prevailed
and Nelson Mandela
walked out of jail.
So keep the faith, baby.
That's the thing to do.
Imani is believing
your dreams will come true.
So when you get up in the morning
or before you go to bed
let four special words
pop out of your head.
Keep the faith, baby
Yeah, Yeah, Yeah!
Keep the faith, baby
Yeah, Yeah, Yeah!

KARAMU

The stories have been told. The storyteller rings her bells and thanks the gathering for listening and joining in. The mother of the house announces: "Let the Karamu begin!" The Karamu is the feast. Kwanzaa has given everyone food for thought. Now they need food for their tummies. Following what the Kwanzaa principles Ujima and Ujamaa teach, each person has brought food to be shared by all. The family invites their friends and honored guests to partake of the mouth-watering salads, breads, stews, and other "eats" placed before them.

After everyone eats, there is more rejoicing and celebrating. Children exchange Kwanzaa cards and play a game, I Got The Spirit!, that helps them to remember the Nguzo Saba, the seven principles of Kwanzaa. Cameras click! Bulbs flash! Folks pose for picture taking.

"*Asante, asante sana!* We thank you, thank you very much," the mother and father say to the gathering. Grandmothers kiss their grandbabies. It is time to say "*Kwaheri,*" which means good-bye.

Happy Kwanzaa to All of You!
And to All a Safe Journey Home.

Now turn the page to learn how you can prepare your own Karamu, make your own Kwanzaa cards and traditional African clothing, and celebrate Kwanzaa in the true spirit of the Nguzo Saba.

Zawadi—Kwanzaa Cards for Friends

Kwanzaa is becoming so popular that Kwanzaa cards and gifts are frequently given. Kwanzaa cards can be purchased or you can design your own. This would make a wonderful Zawadi (gift) for special friends. Many Kwanzaa cards are decorated with African designs, such as drums, masks, sculptures, textile prints, a map of Africa, the Kwanzaa symbols, or a scene depicting a family gathering or African animals.

Kwanzaa Cards

You need:

> construction paper (red, black, and green)
> cardboard paper or white poster paper
> envelopes
> scissors
> markers or crayons, red or green ink pens
> colored tissue paper
> paste (nontoxic)
> buttons, ribbons, yarn, stickers, old jewelry
> photographs
> scraps of African fabric

Use a variety of these items to make your cards.

You do:

Fold a sheet of black construction paper in half.

Cut out a square of red paper and glue it on the front side of the black paper. The red square should be smaller than the black paper.

Cut out a square of green paper and glue it inside the red square. Now you have the three colors of Kwanzaa.

Write or draw a Kwanzaa greeting on the front side.

Decorate the back side of the card and around the Kwanzaa greeting. Cut out a square of white paper and glue it inside the card. Use black, green, and red markers, crayons, or pens to write or draw your Kwanzaa message.

Don't forget to sign your name.

Decorate your envelope. Make sure your envelope is big enough to hold your card. Write your friend's name on the outside of the envelope. Have fun!

I Got the Spirit!—A Kwanzaa Game

I Got the Spirit! is a game of hand clapping, hip shaking, and chanting. The game is designed to promote positive feelings and evoke the spirit of the Kwanzaa principles. The players can make up their own chants to add to the spontaneity of the game.

Players needed: 4 or more (the more the merrier)

Ages: All ages

The players form a circle. A person volunteers or is chosen to be the leader. The leader stands in the middle of the circle. If drummers are present, they can start the rhythm and the players clap to the beat, or the leader starts the hand clapping and the players join in. Everyone dances to the rhythm. The leader chants several times and the players respond. The leader chooses a new leader by dancing in front of him or her. They exchange places and the game continues until everyone is exhausted.

Chant:

LEADER: I got the spirit!
ALL: Hey, Hey!
LEADER: I got the spirit!
ALL: Hey, Hey!
LEADER: I got the spirit!
ALL: Hey, Hey!
LEADER: I got the spirit!
ALL: Hey, Hey!
LEADER: I got Umoja! [*Any of the principles may be used. Since Kujichagulia is a long word, the phrase "I got" does not have to be chanted with it.*]
ALL: Hey, Hey!
LEADER: I got Umoja!
ALL: Hey, Hey!
LEADER: It's in my head.
ALL: Hey, Hey!
LEADER: It's in my feet.
ALL: Hey, Hey!
LEADER: It's in my back.
ALL: Hey, Hey!
LEADER: It's in my heart.
ALL: Hey, Hey!

LEADER: *(dancing ecstatically)* I GOT IT!
ALL: Hey, Hey!
LEADER: I GOT IT!
ALL: Hey, Hey!
LEADER: I GOT IT!
ALL: Hey, Hey!
LEADER: I GOT IT!
ALL: Hey, Hey!
LEADER: *(standing in front of new leader)* YOU TAKE IT!
ALL: Hey, Hey!
NEW LEADER: I GOT THE SPIRIT!
ALL: Hey, Hey!

The hand clapping and the chanting change from fast to faster or slower, loud to louder or softer. Each new leader can change the words to the chant. Flexibility and creativity of the players makes the game fun and exciting. LET THE SPIRIT MOVE YOU!

Looking Good!—
Clothing to Make and Wear

Walking proudly. Heads held high. Children wearing lapas, dashikis, geles, and bubas. An array of hairstyles: cornrows, braids, African curls, and beaded designs adorning heads of happy-faced children. Dashikis are worn by men throughout West, Central, and the southern part of Africa. Bubas are worn by the women of Senegal.

For Those Who Love to Sew

Boy's Sleeveless Dashiki

You need: ¾ yard–1 yard of fabric
(for 6–8-year-old child);
1½ yards for a longer dashiki.

You do: Fold in half for front and for back. Measure 25 inches down on fold, 10¼ inches across the bottom, 9½ inches across the middle, and 6 inches around opened area for arm. Open out front and back at shoulders. Place facing over top and stitch. Trim seams, fold into wrong side, and sew in place by hand or machine.

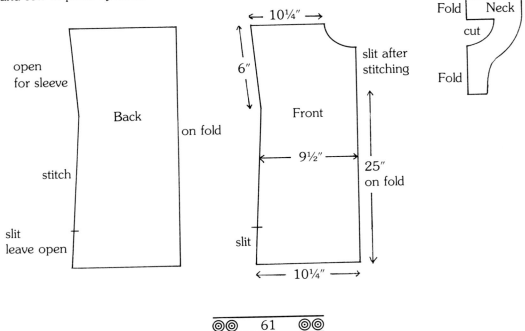

Girl's Full-length Buba

You need: 1½ yards of cloth (for 6–8-year-old child).

You do: Fold fabric in half crosswise. Measure 40″ down from fold.

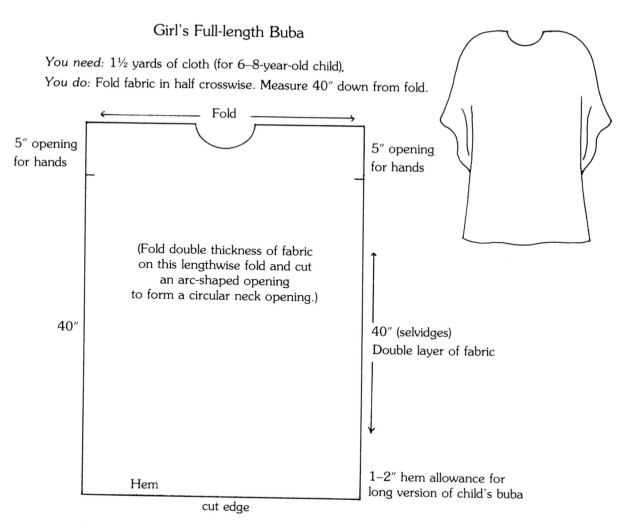

← Fold →

5″ opening for hands

5″ opening for hands

(Fold double thickness of fabric on this lengthwise fold and cut an arc-shaped opening to form a circular neck opening.)

40″

40″ (selvidges)
Double layer of fabric

Hem

cut edge

1–2″ hem allowance for long version of child's buba

Measure 5″ below fold on right and left sides.
Stitch sides together up to that point for hand opening.

Cut circle opening by folding material again lengthwise. Cut out an arc approximately 2½″ over and down from point of fold.

Fold (crosswise)

Fold (lengthwise)

Buba

Fold a 14″ square—or more—piece of fabric in quarters and place it under the buba, and cut out a neck facing as shown above. Place neck facing over neck opening, right sides together. Stitch up ⅛″ seam allowance. Turn to underside and finish. Open out fabric.

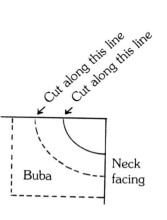

Cut along this line
Cut along this line

Buba

Neck facing

Foods for the Karamu

STEWED CHICKEN AND DUMPLINGS

You need: 3½–4 lbs stewing or roasting chicken, cut up
2 teaspoons salt
DUMPLINGS:
1½ cups all-purpose flour
3 teaspoons baking powder
1 teaspoon salt
¾ cup milk
1 teaspoon minced parsley

You do: Wash chicken pieces carefully and quickly in cold water. Keep in covered bowl in refrigerator until ready to cook. Drain off water that collects in bowl. Fit pieces of chicken compactly in kettle, sprinkle with salt, then barely cover with cold water. Cover with tight lid, heat to boiling, then reduce heat to simmering and cook until tender, 2 to 3 hours. Fifteen minutes before chicken is to be served, add dumplings.

To make the dumplings, sift flour, measure and resift 3 times with baking powder and salt. Add milk and stir just until dry ingredients are dampened; then add parsley and stir until well distributed. Remove cover from stewing chicken. Dip a teaspoon into the liquid, then into the dumpling batter, and drop a spoonful onto the chicken. Drop all dumplings in quickly; then replace cover and boil gently for 12 minutes. Remove dumplings to platter and arrange pieces of chicken around them. Pour the thickened liquid into gravy bowl and serve at table. Makes 5 to 6 servings.

Alice McGill

CANDIED SWEETS

You need: 2 lbs sweet potatoes
4 cups sugar
1 orange, cut up with skin on
1 lemon, cut up with skin on
1 stick butter
1 teaspoon cinnamon
½ teaspoon nutmeg

You do: Peel potatoes and cut into desired serving size. Wash them and place in pot of cold water and cover. Boil potatoes slowly for 20–25 minutes. Pour off most of the water. Add sugar, orange and lemon pieces, butter, cinnamon, and nutmeg. Cook, uncovered, over low flame until sweet potatoes and fruit are candied. The syrup will be clear and juicy. Keep syrup to re-warm any leftovers.

Mary Carter Smith

AFRICAN CHICKEN FROM SIERRA LEONE

You need: 4 medium onions
1 sweet green pepper
6 stalks celery with leaves
peanut or vegetable oil
salt and pepper to taste
2 cut-up frying chickens
about 12 ozs. peanut butter

You do: Coarsely chop onions, green pepper, and celery. Sauté in about 4 tablespoons of oil. Into large pot (preferably iron) pour enough oil for deep-frying (about 2 inches deep). Sprinkle salt and pepper on chicken. Cook in hot oil until done. Remove chicken and pour off oil. Replace chicken in pot and add vegetables. In a separate saucepan slowly add hot water to the peanut butter until it becomes liquified, beating as you mix to prevent lumping. Pour peanut butter liquid into pot with chicken and vegetables. Simmer slowly until tender. Place pot into a larger pan containing water so mixture won't stick. Stir often.

Mary Carter Smith

MOMMA'S BANANA LOAF

You need: 2 bananas
¼ lb butter or margarine
½ cup sugar
Dash vanilla flavoring
2 eggs, separate yolks from the white
1 tablespoon milk
2 cups sifted flour
1 teaspoon baking soda
1 teaspoon salt
1 teaspoon baking powder

You do: Mash bananas. In a separate bowl cream butter or margarine and sugar (add vanilla flavoring) until light. Beat egg yolks and add to butter and sugar. Stir in bananas and milk. Sift dry ingredients together and beat into creamed mixture. Beat egg whites until stiff, and fold into batter. Pour into greased bread pan. Bake for one hour at 350°F.

LATINO KWANZAA BEANS AND RICE

Throughout Latin American countries such as Cuba and Brazil black beans and rice dishes are a must.

You need: 1 cup chopped green onions
1 cup chopped green pepper
1 cup chopped red pepper
2 cloves garlic, crushed
2 cups water
2 tablespoons olive oil
1 can chopped tomatoes or stewed tomatoes
1 teaspoon vinegar, or suitable to taste
2 16 oz. cans black beans
Dash of salt or suitable to taste
Dash of hot pepper
½ teaspoon oregano
3 cups cooked rice (hot)

You do: Sauté onions, peppers, and garlic in olive oil until tender; stir in tomatoes. Add a little water, vinegar, beans, and seasonings. Simmer until heated through. Serve over rice. Serves 6.

KUUMBA SALAD (RED, BLACK, AND GREEN)

As you know, Kuumba means creativity. Create your own salad for Kwanzaa by mixing together seven different vegetables and/or fruits that are red, black, and green, the Kwanzaa colors. Choose from the following:

Red	Black	Green
tomatoes	olives	lettuce
apples	raisins	kiwi
strawberries	grapes	honeydew melon
radishes	black beans (drained)	cucumbers
cherries	dates	avocados
plums	prunes	green peppers
red peppers	black cherries	green beans
red cabbage	eggplant	peas
red onions		pears
kidney beans		green olives

	pimientos		grapes
	mangoes		celery
	peaches		spinach
	raspberries		broccoli
	grapes		zucchini
	watermelon		watermelon
Seasonings:	paprika	pepper	basil
	cayenne pepper (dash)		oregano
Seasonings for fruit:	cinnamon		
	nutmeg		
	cloves		
DRESSING:	red vinegar and oil		cucumber and dill

SWEET FRUIT DRESSING

Mix together 1 cup of strawberry yogurt, dashes of ginger, nutmeg, cinnamon, and juice of ½ lemon. Chill.

JAMAICAN CARROT JUICE

You need: two bags carrots
water
1 can condensed milk
1 teaspoon vanilla flavoring
1½ teaspoons nutmeg
1 teaspoon cinnamon

You do: Place carrots, a few at a time, in blender. Add water as needed. Strain the blended carrots in a strainer with small holes or squeeze the juice through a cheesecloth into a large bowl. Add remaining ingredients. Stir thoroughly and pour into pitcher. Chill for 1 hour.

Nadya Harris

Musical Notes—Kwanzaa Songs to Sing

THIS LITTLE LIGHT

This lit-tle light of mine I'm gon-na let it shine. This lit-tle light of mine

I'm gon-na let it shine._____ This lit - tle light of mine__

I'm gon-na let it shine. Let it shine.__ Let it shine. Let it shine.__

Eve-ry - where I go__ I'm gon-na let it shine. Eve - ry - where I go__

I'm gon-na let it shine._____ Eve - ry - where I go__

I'm gon-na let it shine. Let it shine.__ Let it shine. Let it shine.__

WE ARE PULLING TOGETHER

We are pull - ing to -geth - er. We are pull - ing to -geth - er.

We are pull - ing to -geth - er. Oh yes we are.

IT'S KWANZAA TIME

Call your Fa - ther! Call your Moth - er! Call your Sis - ter!

Call your Broth - er! It's Kwan - zaa time._ Fam - i - ly time. It's

Kwan - zaa time. Fam - i - ly time. Black peo - ple pull - ing to - geth - er, Ha - ram - bee

Try - ing to make things bet - ter, Ha - ram - bee Sev - en days and sev - en nights

Sev - en can - dles we_ will light _ Sev - en can - dles we_ will light._

Green is for the land. Red is for the blood. Black is for the peo - ple

whom we love. It's Kwan - zaa time._ Fam - i - ly time. It's

Kwan - zaa time.___ Fam - i - ly time.___ The

CONTRIBUTORS

Nana Yaa Asantewa (Gloria Bivens) wrote the song "We Are Pulling Together." A storyteller from Louisville, Kentucky, she is known for "shaking up" and "waking up" the audiences at the National Festival of Black Storytelling with her singing and dancing.

Eloise Greenfield wrote the book *Rosa Parks*. Ms. Greenfield is an award-winning author from Washington, D.C. She has written more than thirty books, including *Honey, I Love* and *Nathaniel Talking,* a Coretta Scott King Award winner.

Nadya Harris contributed the recipe Jamaican Carrot Juice from her collection of family recipes. Ms. Harris is a storyteller from Philadelphia, Pennsylvania.

Kathleen Kilpatrick transcribed the songs "We Are Pulling Together," "It's Kwanzaa Time," and "This Little Light." Ms. Kilpatrick is a flutist and music teacher with the school district of Philadelphia.

Alice McGill contributed the recipe Stewed Chicken and Dumplings. A storyteller living in Columbia, Maryland, Ms. McGill is known for her stunning, dramatic portrayal of Sojourner Truth, and her album, "The Flying African."

Tejumola Ologboni contributed the Yoruba libation. A storyteller, poet, and master drummer known for his electrifying performances from Milwaukee, Wisconsin, Mr. Ologboni won the 1986 Tall-Tellers contest at the National Festival of Black Storytelling, held in Chicago.

Mary Carter Smith collected the Candied Sweets recipe from her grandmother and the African Chicken from Sierra Leone recipe from an African friend. She is a leading pioneer in contemporary storytelling and the co-founder of *In the Tradition*, the National Festival of Black Storytelling, and the National Association of Black Storytellers.

Carole Weathers designed the dashiki and buba clothing. A weaver living in Philadelphia, Pennsylvania, Ms. Weathers has studied with the Navajo Indians. Her favorite hobby is playing the cello.